THE MAGICIAN'S SECRET

ZACHARY HYMAN

illustrated by

JOE BLUHM

tundra

For my friends and family, with love. "Whatever you believe, you can achieve!" —**ZH**

This is for all the travelers, dreamers and storytellers, and especially for my grandfather, Howard Borel Jr.—the great twentieth-century man —**JB**

Text and illustrations copyright © 2018 by Stuart Hyman/Three Lions Enterprises

Tundra Books, an imprint of Penguin Random House Canada Young Readers, a Penguin Random House Company

Library and Archives Canada Cataloguing in Publication

Hyman, Zachary, author
     The magician's secret / Zachary Hyman ; illustrated by Joe Bluhm.

Issued in print and electronic formats.
ISBN 978-1-77049-894-5 (hardback).—ISBN 978-1-77049-896-9 (epub)

     I. Bluhm, Joe, 1980-, illustrator II. Title.

PS8615.Y527M34 2017   jC813'.6   C2016-900976-9
                                                C2016-900977-7

Published simultaneously in the United States of America by Tundra Books of Northern New York, an imprint of Penguin Random House Canada Young Readers, a Penguin Random House Company

Library of Congress Control Number: 2017939198

Edited by Janice Weaver
Designed by Andrew Roberts
The artwork in this book was rendered digitally.
The text was set in Bookman Old Style.

Printed and bound in Canada

www.penguinrandomhouse.ca

2   3   4   5   22   21   20   19   18

"**B**e a good boy tonight," said Mom, crossing her arms against the cold.

"Don't worry, dear. Charlie's always a good boy," replied Grandpa with a wink.

"Dad, please make sure he gets to bed early this time," she pleaded. "No more hocus-pocus!"

Grandpa was like a big kid who never grew up. He played games with me, and he let me eat ice cream and cookies and candy.

He also knew the most amazing tricks, because he used to be a magician. He knew how to pull a rabbit from a hat and make a coin disappear. He would *never* tell me how he did it, though. He always said that was a magician's secret.

But what I loved most of all were his wonderful stories . . .

Grandpa's tales all began at his Magic Story Chest. This was a great big wooden trunk hidden in the darkest, most cobwebby corner of the attic. Each time he told me a story, Grandpa would blow the dust off that old chest, open the heavy lid with a bone-rattling creak and reach in for something special he had picked up on one of his adventures.

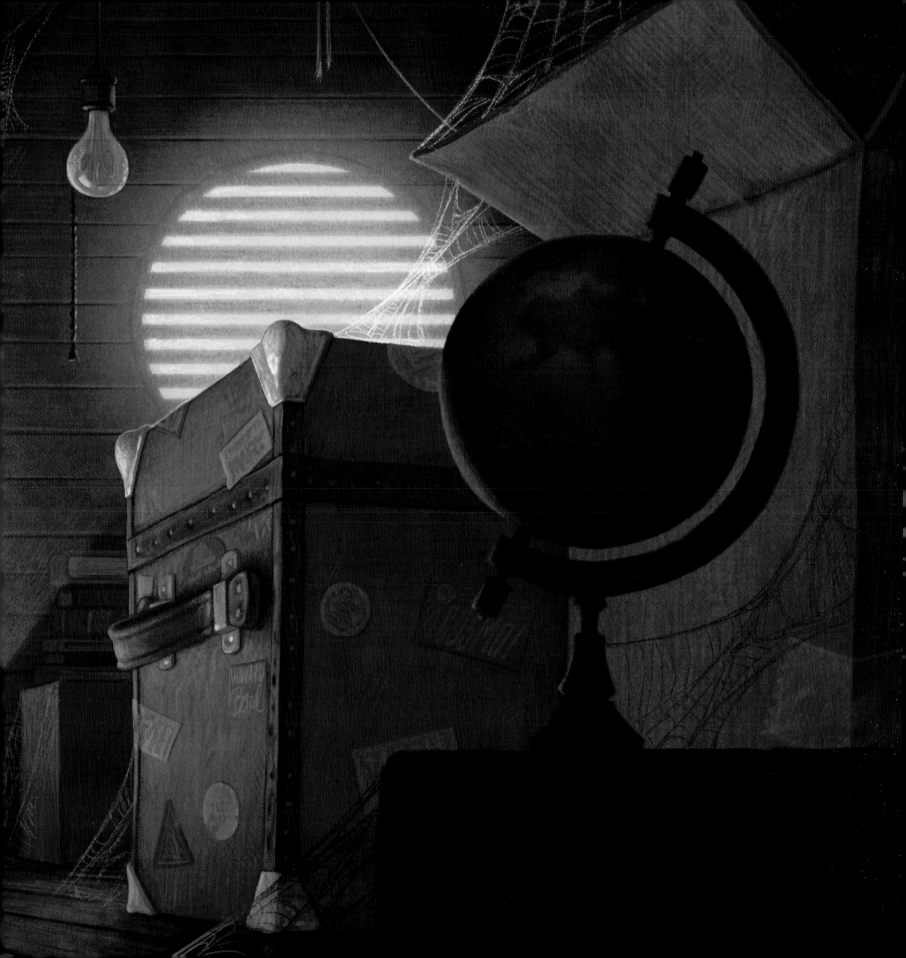

That night, Grandpa reached way down into the chest and pulled out an hourglass filled with glistening sand.

"This sand is from the burial tomb of Tut, the boy king," he whispered.

He handed it to me so I could have a closer look. I swear I could still feel the heat of that mighty Egyptian sun!

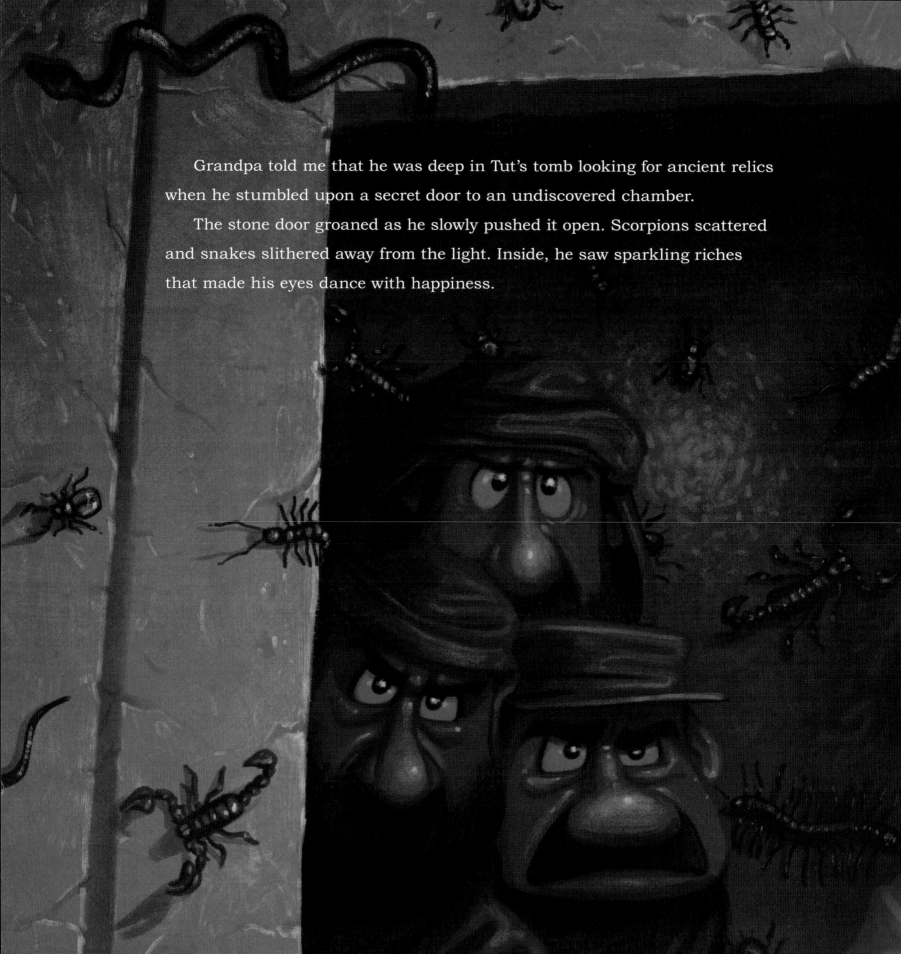

Grandpa told me that he was deep in Tut's tomb looking for ancient relics when he stumbled upon a secret door to an undiscovered chamber.

The stone door groaned as he slowly pushed it open. Scorpions scattered and snakes slithered away from the light. Inside, he saw sparkling riches that made his eyes dance with happiness.

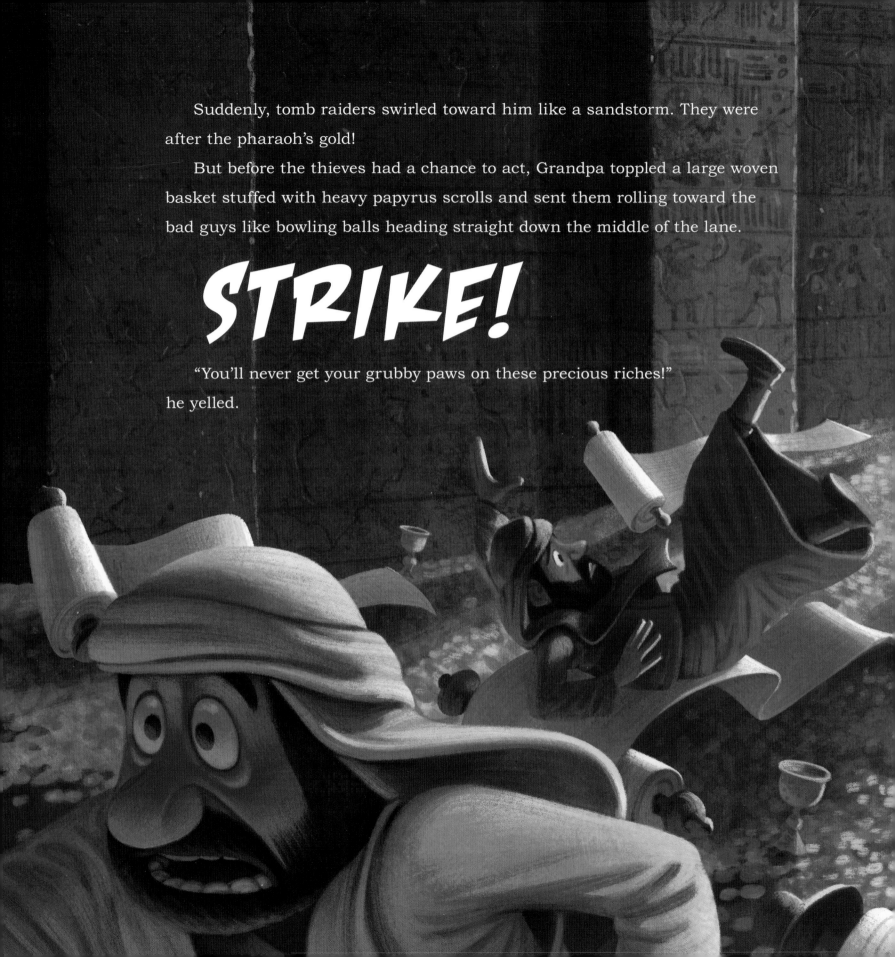

Suddenly, tomb raiders swirled toward him like a sandstorm. They were after the pharaoh's gold!

But before the thieves had a chance to act, Grandpa toppled a large woven basket stuffed with heavy papyrus scrolls and sent them rolling toward the bad guys like bowling balls heading straight down the middle of the lane.

STRIKE!

"You'll never get your grubby paws on these precious riches!" he yelled.

I couldn't wait to hear more of Grandpa's stories.

One fine and fair spring evening, he went to the old trunk and pulled out a long white scarf.

"This belonged to the Red Baron, the great First World War fighter pilot," he explained. "He was the ace of aces—the most feared man alive."

Grandpa told me that he once got into a real dogfight with the Red Baron, high up in the skies over France.

RAT-A-TAT-TAT!

The sound of the Red Baron's machine-gun fire ripped through the sky. The Baron was so close that Grandpa could see the mad look in his eyes.

"Hope you like to swim!" the German shouted as he squeezed the trigger once more.

Grandpa put his plane into a steep
dive, and the Red Baron followed as if
it was a game of cat and mouse. They
plunged toward some shimmering water,
but Grandpa managed to pull up at the
last second . . .

SPLASH!

The Red Baron wasn't so lucky. He took
a swan dive into the waves.

As Grandpa flew past for one last look,
he snatched the Red Baron's scarf from
the sky.

"I'll take that!" he said, escaping into
the clouds with a grin.

One hot and steamy summer evening, Grandpa showed me a curious object from his Magic Story Chest.

"Is this some kind of fuzzy baseball?" I asked, turning it over in my hands.

Grandpa laughed. "It's a coconut shell, Charlie. I found it when I was exploring a beautiful tropical beach."

He told me that he had been dozing under the shade of a towering palm tree when he was woken up by a thunderous . . .

ROAARRR!

Looming over him was a giant *Tyrannosaurus rex*—and he hadn't come for the coconuts!

The snarling, slobbering dinosaur inched closer and closer, licking his lips and snapping his massive jaws. Grandpa was going to make a nice light snack.

"Oh no!" he pleaded. "Trust me, I'm not very yummy!"

But the *T. rex* kept coming . . .

ZING! ZING! ZING!

Suddenly, dozens of rocks rained down through the air, scaring the nasty dinosaur away.

"Thank you! Thank you very much!" shouted Grandpa, peering up at the top of the cliff.

But he always stopped the story right there. Who saved my grandpa? He said that was for me to figure out.

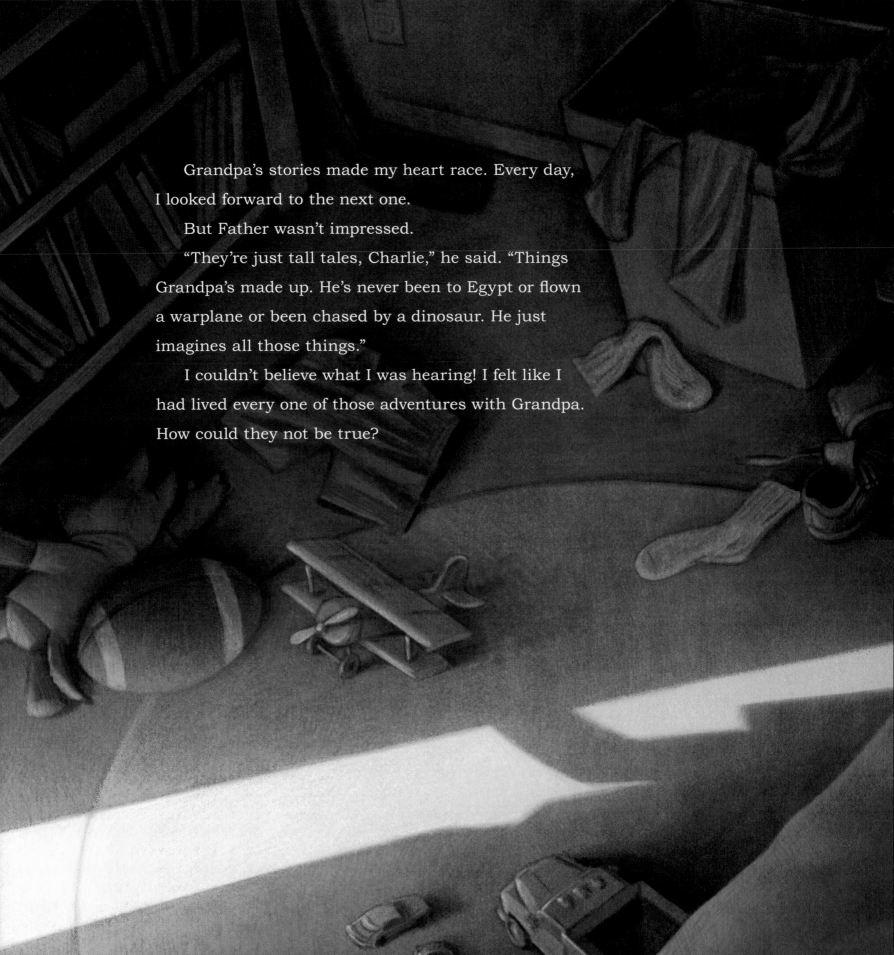

Grandpa's stories made my heart race. Every day,
I looked forward to the next one.

But Father wasn't impressed.

"They're just tall tales, Charlie," he said. "Things
Grandpa's made up. He's never been to Egypt or flown
a warplane or been chased by a dinosaur. He just
imagines all those things."

I couldn't believe what I was hearing! I felt like I
had lived every one of those adventures with Grandpa.
How could they not be true?

I went to find Grandpa in his room.

"Father says your stories are only make-believe," I stammered. "I thought you were telling me the truth!"

Grandpa breathed a deep and heavy sigh. "You know the problem with grown-ups, Charlie? They don't have faith in make-believe anymore. And that's too bad, because when you use your imagination, you can turn a dream into something real."

"You can?"

"Why, sure! We've done it over and over again, with cameras and computers, automobiles and airplanes. We've traveled into space and explored the deepest oceans. We've even landed on the moon!

"The imagination is the most powerful force in the world. Magic is all around us, kiddo—in me and in you. All you need to do is believe. You know what I like to say? Whatever you believe, you can achieve!"

Grandpa pulled up his sleeves and held out his palms to show me they were empty. Then he waved his hands as fast as he could and . . .

Presto!

I was staring at two tightly closed fists.

"Which one?" he asked.

I bit my lip and tapped his left hand. What was Grandpa's secret?

He opened his fingers one by one, and I saw . . .

"A rock?" I said, taking it from his hand.

"Oh, this isn't just any old rock, Charlie. This is the philosopher's stone—it can do magical things."

"Like what?"

"It can make sick men healthy and old men young. It can make poor people rich beyond their wildest dreams. But do you know the most amazing thing about this special stone?"

I shook my head. I was too awestruck to speak.

"It looks like any other old rock on the ground. The philosopher's stone is everywhere—in every field and under every tree." Grandpa pulled me close. "But to be able to *see* it, you have to *believe* it."

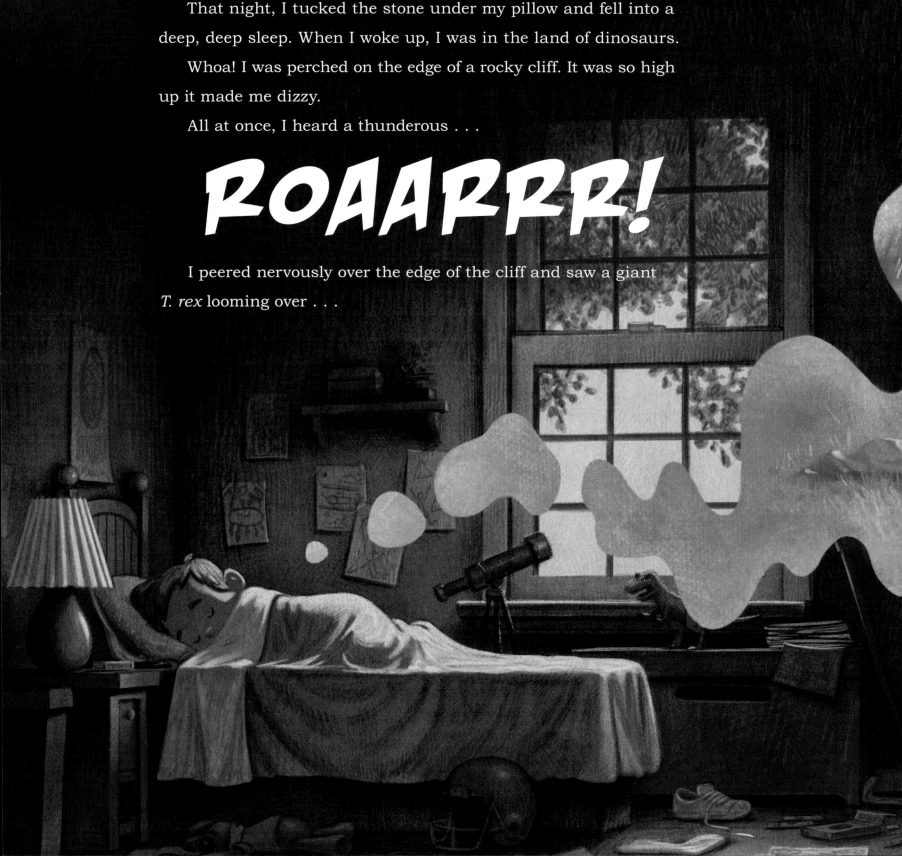

That night, I tucked the stone under my pillow and fell into a deep, deep sleep. When I woke up, I was in the land of dinosaurs.

Whoa! I was perched on the edge of a rocky cliff. It was so high up it made me dizzy.

All at once, I heard a thunderous . . .

ROAARRR!

I peered nervously over the edge of the cliff and saw a giant *T. rex* looming over . . .

Grandpa?!

"Well, don't just stand there, kiddo!" he shouted,
waving his hands in the air. "Help me!"

I looked down at the rock I had clutched in my
fist and knew exactly what I had to do . . .